I Can't Sleep!

For my son Louis

This edition first published in 2017 by Gecko Press
PO Box 9335, Marion Square, Wellington 6141, New Zealand
info@geckopress.com

English language edition © Gecko Press Ltd 2017
Translation © Sarah Ardizzone 2017

Original title: *Non Pas Dodo!*
Text and illustrations by Stephanie Blake
© 2005 l'école des loisirs, Paris

Distributed in the United Kingdom by Bounce Sales and Marketing, www.bouncemarketing.co.uk
Distributed in Australia by Scholastic Australia, www.scholastic.com.au
Distributed in New Zealand by Upstart Distribution, www.upstartpress.co.nz

Edited by Penelope Todd
Typesetting by Vida & Luke Kelly, New Zealand
Printed in China by Everbest Printing Co. Ltd, an accredited ISO 14001 & FSC certified printer

Hardback ISBN: 978-1-776571-63-5
Paperback ISBN: 978-1-776571-64-2

For more curiously good books, visit www.geckopress.com

Stephanie Blake

I Can't Sleep!

Translated by Sarah Ardizzone

GECKO PRESS

One day
Simon
and
his little brother
Casper
decided to
build a
MEGA
GIGA-NORMOUS
hut.

When they found exactly
the right spot,
Simon
explained
his building plan.

"We'll take the BIG blanket
and hang it over there,"
said Simon.

"Hangit ober dere!"
shouted Casper.

"Our hut is
STUPENDOUS!"
said Simon.

"**STUPIDOUS!**"
Casper shouted.

Night was falling.

"Come on, Casper,
it's time for dinner.
Tomorrow morning, we'll come back
very
very
very
early
to finish our hut."

That night,
Simon and Casper
went to bed dreaming of
the big day
they'd have tomorrow.

But suddenly,
blink-blink!

Casper opened his eyes…

"Wheresmyblanky?
Intahut!
I want
BLANKY!"

Simon thought a minute.
Then he said:
"We can't get your blanky,
Casper, it's too dark."

"Can't sleep without blanky,"
explained Casper.

"There's no blanky. Lie down
or I'll get cross!" said Simon.

"NO BLANKY?
NO BED!"
screamed Casper.

Simon
decided to help
his little brother.
"Casper! Bring me my cape.
I'm going to find
your
blanky!"

"Me come too," said Casper.

"No, Casper, you're too little,
you wait here."

And Simon went out
into the dark,
dark night.

The first thing
Simon noticed
was the cold.
And the ground was a little damp.
So he ran a little faster.
Pitter-pat, pitter-pat
went
his
steps
in
the
night.

When Simon reached the
GIGA-NORMOUS
hut,
he found Casper's blanky.
He felt
so
proud.
He was
Super Rabbit.
Or even
Super Mega Rabbit.
And he was afraid of
nothing!

With a spring in his step,
he headed home.
But then, right behind him,
he heard a noise,
or rather a breath.
Someone breathing!

"It's the wind, of course.
Silly me! I'm not scared
of a breath of wind!"

But Simon wasn't reassured.

He thought he saw
something moving, close by
in the dark.

And when he turned around...

There was a
MEGA
GIGA-NORMOUS
MONSTER
ready to gobble him up.

"CAAAASSPERRRR!"
Simon screamed, and

he ran

and ran

and ran

so fast that...

before
he knew it,
he was
home.

And for the rest of the night
Simon told
Casper
about his extraordinary adventure.
And
Casper
felt
very
very
very
proud
to have a
big brother like Simon.

The next day
at breakfast
their mother
was very surprised
to find
two
little
rabbits…
fast
asleep.